ARE WE THERE YET, DADDY?

by
Virginia Walters
illustrated by S.D. Schindler

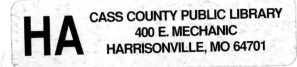

VIKING
Published by the Penguin Group
Penguin Putnam Books for Young Readers, 345 Hudson Street, New York, New York 10014, U.S.A.
Penguin Books Ltd, 27 Wrights Lane, London W8 5TZ, England
Penguin Books Australia Ltd, Ringwood, Victoria, Australia
Penguin Books Canada Ltd, 10 Alcorn Avenue, Toronto, Ontario, Canada M4V 3B2
Penguin Books (N.Z.) Ltd, 182-190 Wairau Road, Auckland 10, New Zealand

Penguin Books Ltd, Registered Offices: Harmondsworth, Middlesex, England

First published in 1999 by Viking, a member of Penguin Putnam Books for Young Readers

1 3 5 7 9 10 8 6 4 2

Text copyright © Virginia Walters, 1999
Illustrations copyright © S.D. Schindler, 1999
All rights reserved

LIBRARY OF CONGRESS CATALOGING-IN-PUBLICATION DATA
Walters, Virginia.
Are we there yet, Daddy? / Virginia Walters ; illustrated by S. D. Schindler.
p. cm.
Summary: A young boy describes the trip he and his father make to
Grandma's house, measuring how many miles are left at various points on the trip.
ISBN 0-670-87402-7
[1. Automobile travel—Fiction. 2. Fathers and sons—Fiction.
3. Stories in rhyme.] I. Schindler, S. D., ill. II. Title.
PZ8.3.W197Ar 1999 [E]—dc21   97-18220 CIP AC

Printed in Hong Kong
Set in Usherwood

To Steven and David,
who frequently asked, and Ron,
who patiently responded to,
"Are we there yet, Daddy?"
—V.W.

◆ ◆ ◆

To Sue, Carl, Andrea, Bubby, and Rusty at Otter Pond.
—S.D.S.

Going to my grandma's house, it's so far away.
Going to my grandma's house, we're going today.

Put the map in my lap.
It will show the way.

"Are we there yet, Daddy?"
 Daddy says, "*No.*"
"How much farther do we have to go?"
        "Just look at the map, Son.
          Then you will know."
          We have **100** more miles to go.

Going down the highway, mile after mile.
Going down the highway, singing makes us smile.
Dad and I and Bitsy leave the city
For a while.

"Are we there yet, Daddy?"
Daddy says, "*No.*"
"How much farther do we have to go?"
"Just look at the map, Son.
Then you will know."
We have **90** more miles to go.

Racing with a freight train, count the cars real fast.
Racing with a freight train, wave as it goes past.
The engineer signals clear
And gives the horn a blast.

"Are we there yet, Daddy?"
 Daddy says, "*No*."
"How much farther do we have to go?"
        "Just look at the map, Son.
        Then you will know."
        We have **80** more miles to go.

Going on a bumpy road, a long way out of town.
Going on a bumpy road, I'm bouncing up and down.
Bounce high, bounce low, bounce fast, bounce slow.
Uh-oh, I see Dad frown!

"Are we there yet, Daddy?"
 Daddy says, "*No.*"
"How much farther do we have to go?"
        "Just look at the map, Son.
        Then you will know."
        We have **70** more miles to go.

Going over bridges where rapid rivers flow.
Going over bridges, please tell me if you know:
Why do currents whirl, and ripples curl,
And where does water go?

"Are we there yet, Daddy?"
Daddy says, *"No."*
"How much farther do we have to go?"
"Just look at the map, Son.
Then you will know."
We have **60** more miles to go.

Going through a forest, tall trees all around.
Going through a forest, shadows on the ground.
An autumn breeze blows falling leaves
Of red and gold and brown.

"Are we there yet, Daddy?"
Daddy says, "*No*."
"How much farther do we have to go?"
    "Just look at the map, Son.
    Then you will know."
    We have **50** more miles to go.

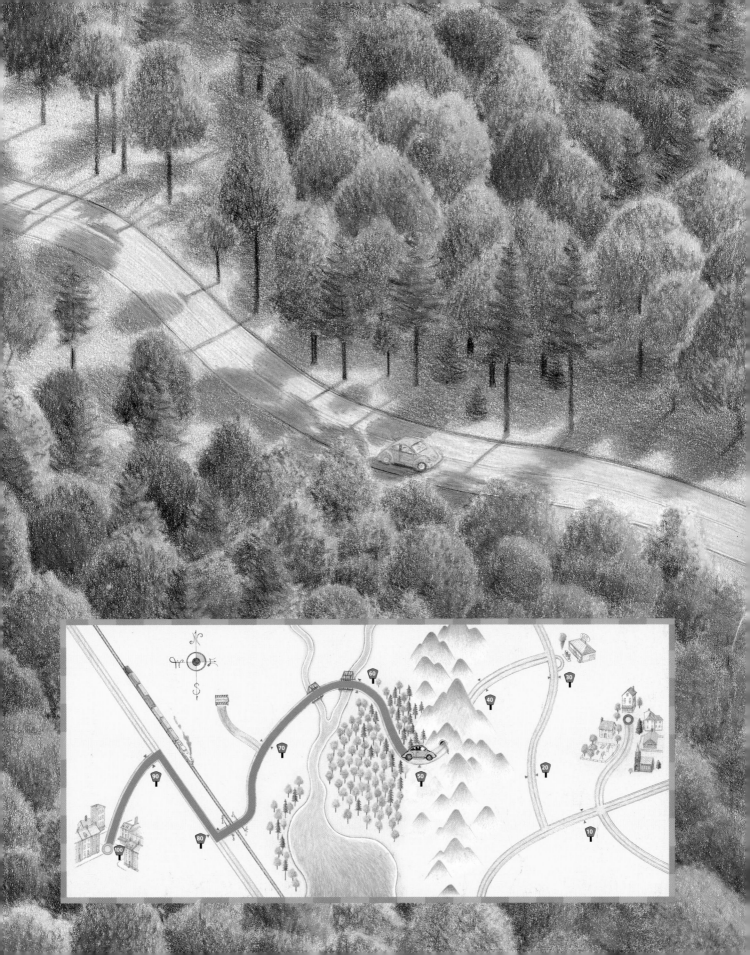

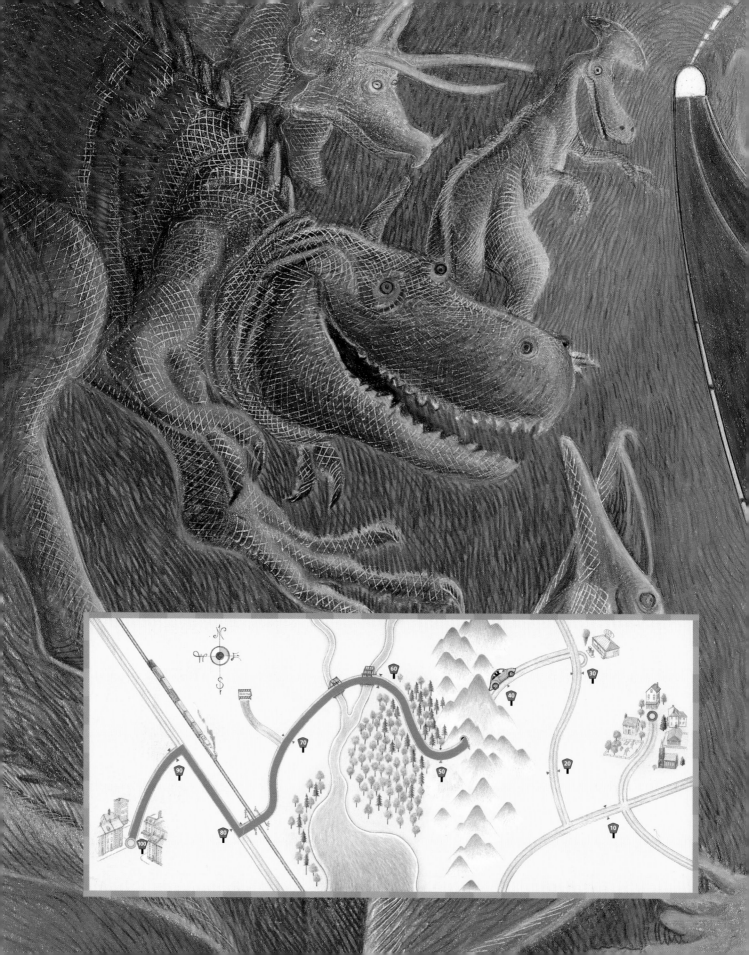

Entering a tunnel that isn't very wide.
Entering a tunnel, it's really dark inside.
This could be where secretly
The dinosaurs still hide.

"Are we there yet, Daddy?"
Daddy says, "*No.*"
"How much farther do we have to go?"
"Just look at the map, Son.
Then you will know."
We have **40** more miles to go.

Stopping at a minimart to get a bite to eat.
Stopping at a minimart, I get an ice-cream treat.
Dad gets upset because I get
Some chocolate on the seat.

"Are we there yet, Daddy?"
Daddy says, "*No.*"
"How much farther do we have to go?"

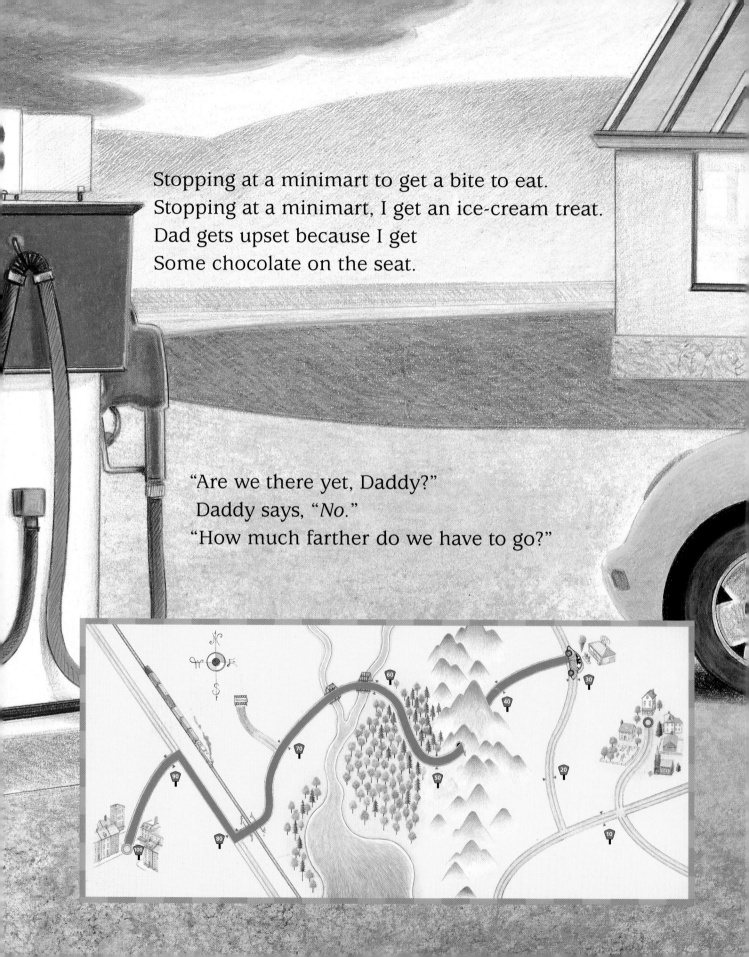

"Just look at the map, Son.
Then you will know."
We have **30** more miles to go.

Going through a rainstorm, windshield wipers swishing.
Going through a rainstorm, raindrops splashing-splishing.
Lightning flashes, thunder crashes.
Now I'm rainbow wishing.

"Are we there yet, Daddy?"
  Daddy says, "*No.*"
"How much farther do we have to go?"
    "Just look at the map, Son.
    Then you will know."
    We have **20** more miles to go.

Going fast past other cars,
with their motors roaring.
Going slow past other cars,
this is getting boring.
It's hard to keep from going to sleep,
And I hear Bitsy snoring.

"Are we there yet, Daddy?"
Daddy says, "*No.*"
"How much farther do we have to go?"
      "Just look at the map, Son.
      Then you will know."
      We have just **10** more miles to go.

Going down some quiet streets, passing by a park.
Going down some quiet streets, it is getting dark.
The town clock chimes so many times
That it makes Bitsy bark.

"Are we there yet, Daddy?"
Daddy says, "*Yes.*"
We don't have farther to go, I guess.

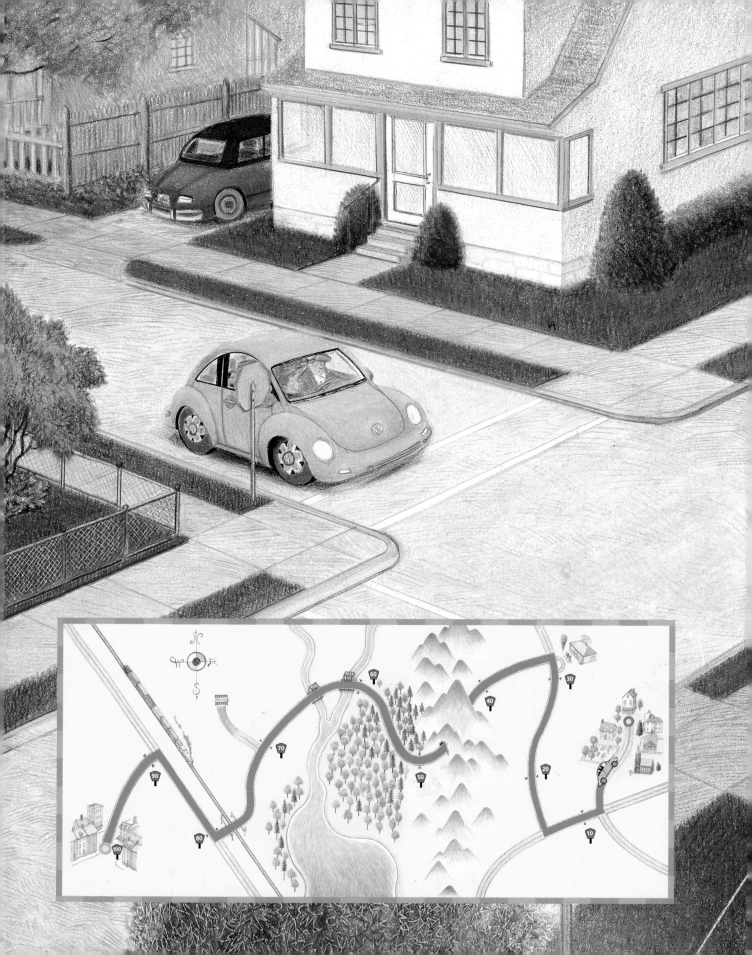